Tomorrow, When I Die

Tomorrow, When I Die

A Christmas Adventure

KAREN J CARLISLE

Kraken Publishing

Tomorrow when I Die: A Christmas Adventure

A catalogue record for this book is available from the National Library of Australia

ISBN: 978-0-6458151-3-9
Series: Carlisle, Karen J.

This is a Viola Stewart Christmas story, also published in the third story collection of *The Adventures of Viola Stewart, The Illusioneer & Other Tales*.
Also available separately as eBook.

This book is written in British English.
Printed in Australia.
Typeset in Times Roman 11pt.

Published by Kraken Publishing.
www.krakenpublishing.com

For those who love Christmas stories,
Those who love mysteries,
And David,
for his support and encouragement
(even on my bad days).

Contents

Chapter One

The Chronic Argonauts

The midday sun streamed across the kitchen table. Viola plunged the wooden spoon into the pudding bowl, with a satisfying squelch. She licked her lips and stirred the thick mixture.

Bowls clattered behind her. Polly hummed quietly. Viola closed her eye and smiled. It was the same tune her mother used to hum.

"Oh, why can't we have Christmas more often?" She plopped another sixpence into the mixture.

Polly raised an eyebrow. "Isn't one sixpence more traditional?"

"Sir Archibald will be disappointed if he misses out again this year." Viola inhaled the sweet smell of candied orange peel, currants and brown sugar. She dunked her finger into the concoction and licked her fingertip. "A little more nutmeg, I think?"

Polly dipped a teaspoon into the spice tin and dusted nutmeg over the fruit mixture. She scooped the pudding onto the cloth, gathered up the corners and knotted them.

"Will Doctor Collins will be well enough to join you for Christmas Eve?" Polly slipped the parcel onto a wooden dowel and lowered it into a pot of boiling water. "It's been weeks since the accident."

"He's lucky he didn't shatter the bone," replied Viola. Taking irrational and unnecessary risks. Again. She'd had everything under control until Henry decided she needed rescuing. Her heart ached. *He could have died!*

Polly frowned.

"Sir Archibald has ordered him to rest up until Lady Calthorpe's party," said Viola. "He's engineered a contraption to help with manoeuvrability." Shadows across the table faded as grey clouds crept across the sky. "Looks like rain."

"And the forecast had been for fine weather for the party." Polly sighed. "I do hope it doesn't spoil afternoon tea with Doctor Collins."

"He'll cope until the festivities tomorrow night." Viola flexed her fingers. "He's driving me to distraction. Every afternoon, the same questions. He wants to know every detail about my day."

"He is very fond of you, Miss." Polly's cheeks flushed.

Viola gazed out of the kitchen window and tracked the clouds as they blocked the sun. He's worried I'll go off on an adventure without him. Why can't he trust me? She clenched her hands. I suspect he has Sir Archibald keeping watch on me.

"Am I not as able as any man?" she whispered. Perhaps she should go on an adventure, by herself, just to show him?

Polly cleared her throat. "He is fortunate you were there, Miss."

Viola picked up a stray currant from the bench and popped it in her mouth.

"I'll only want a light supper tonight, Polly. I think I'll settle in with a good book after I return from afternoon tea."

"A new Sherlock Holmes?" Polly's eyes lit up.

"No," replied Viola. "Sir Archibald has promised me something new this afternoon. Doctor Doyle calls it science fantasy. It's a fantastical tale about a man in search of his true time."

A loud pounding echoed down the hall from the front doorway. Viola glanced at the small clock on the wall. Two o'clock.

"Are you expecting any visitors, Miss?" Polly dusted her floury hands on her apron and yanked it off.

Viola shook her head, arranged her skirts and followed Polly into the entry hall. Polly straightened her cap and opened the door.

Sir Archibald bustled into the hall, his cheeks flushed. His gaze darted along the hall until he spotted Viola. His spectacles jiggled precariously on the tip of his nose as he puffed. Polly stepped back and caught his coat and cane as he tossed them aside.

"Has something happened?" Viola's heart sank. "Is it Henry?"

Sir Archibald shook his head and caught his breath.

"Polly, get Sir Archibald a brandy."

Polly bobbed and skittered down the hall.

"What's happened, Sir Archibald?" Viola placed her hand on his shoulder.

"It's... I've been... oh, God." Deep furrows etched his forehead; he leaned against the wall. "Viola, you must help me." He looked her in the eye. "Tomorrow, I'm going to die."

Viola observed Sir Archibald as she wrapped a blanket around his shoulders. The soles of his shoes were scuffed, the cuff of his trousers torn. His face was still pale and his gaze darted around the room, lingering on the door and window, never meeting Viola's eye.

"You've had enough brandy," she said.

"What would you do?" he mumbled. "If the fate of the Empire rested on it?"

Viola frowned and added four spoons of sugar to his drink. "Drink your tea. It will clear your head."

"I don't want to die." Sir Archibald's tea cup rattled on its saucer. He clenched his hands but still they trembled. "But if it's for the good of the Empire...?" His hand clasped his inside jacket pocket.

"You can't possibly know you will die tomorrow," said Viola. His mind was still muddled. She placed her palm on his forehead. No fever. "How long were you wandering about last night?" She checked his pulse.

"I've seen the future, Viola."

Viola shook her head. *Impossible.*

"It's like the Chronic Argonaut." Sir Archibald gulped his tea.

"The–?"

"That story by the school teacher. I was going to give you a copy this afternoon." He removed Viola's hand from his wrist. "Do you believe in travelling through time?"

Viola's eye widened. "Surely the science is unachievable?"

"There was a closed lecture on temporal displacement, by a Professor Black, at one of the regular Research Meetings," replied Sir Archibald.

"But the amount of energy required would be astronomical. The cost alone would be prohibitive."

"I have irrefutable proof. I wasn't supposed to bring anything back with me." He leaned forward clutching at his jacket. "Too dangerous. Could change everything. But I had to."

A corner of crumpled paper peeked out from under his jacket. Viola seized the folded paper and flipped it open.

THE TIMES
24th December, 1889.
Queen's Traitor Physician Shot Dead After Assassinating Queen.
Sir Archibald Huntington-Smythe, prominent biomechanical surgeon and personal physician to Her Majesty betrays sacred trust.

"But that's impossible."

"Just improbable." Sir Archibald snatched back the newspaper and shoved it in his pocket. "But, I assure you, it is real."

"But..." She sat down beside him. "Surely there's been a misunderstanding? Perhaps if you return the newspaper, change your actions? That would create an alternate future and avoid–?"

"No." Sir Archibald shook his head. "I cannot go back, or forward, to mend my mistakes. Professor Black won't let me travel again."

"Then what is the point of knowing such events if one can't change them?" asked Viola.

"The Professor said he could help. He is expecting me tomorrow. I wandered all night, trying to think of another way." Sir Archibald pushed his spectacles up his nose. "He requires information about The Queen. Private things. Things covered by the Secrets Act. But I can't... How can I trust them? I can't tell them..." He swallowed and spoke quickly. "Better to die than be branded a traitor."

"You're not a traitor."

"And therefore I must die tomorrow. Unless..." A faint smile flickered over his lips. "That is why I am here." He clasped Viola's hand in his. "I need your help."

Viola raised an eyebrow.

"We can prevent it," said Sir Archibald. "Perhaps, if you can find the true traitor, and prove who is behind the assassination? I won't need to die or, if it is still my fate, then it will not be for nothing."

"Does Henry know?" she asked. He was Sir Archibald's best friend. Surely he would help?

"No, he can barely walk without assistance." Sir Archibald shook his head. "And I don't trust anyone's detectiving but yours. You must travel in my place. Only you could solve this conundrum, Viola."

Viola shifted in her chair. It seemed simple enough. At its heart, it was a causality logic puzzle, but with the added complication of time travel. She smiled. And she was unknown to the Professor, so he wouldn't suspect her of subterfuge. Except... Her shoulders slumped.

"But they will recognise this." Her fingers skimmed over her eye patch. "All of West London knows of the 'one-eyed doctor'."

Sir Archibald smiled. "I've thought of that. How do you feel about disguises?" he asked.

"Disguises?"

"Professor Marchland, one of the Research Meeting fraternity, died last month in a laboratory accident. It was he who introduced me to Professor Black and his temporal machine. I may have mentioned his sister, and research partner, had returned from the continent to sort out his estate. They've never met her." He turned his tea cup on the saucer. "Professor Marchland wished to bequeath money to a worthy research cause. And Professor Black is in need of funds for further research." He grinned. "They are expecting her tomorrow at three o'clock."

"She helped in his research?"

Sir Archibald nodded.

"I can wear my tinted spectacles." Viola sat on the edge of her seat. "I could say I was injured in the accident, damaged my eyes, and have photophobia." Yes, that could work.

"Excellent." Sir Archibald sipped his tea. "Then it's settled. There's a vacant house across the street. I'll wait there until you return."

"No," said Viola. ""We need to keep you safe. You must stay here. I insist. Then afternoon tea with Henry. All will be well. "

"But you can't go alone–"

"What choice do you have?" asked Viola. "Trust me, Sir Archibald. You shall be partying tomorrow night with the rest of us."

Viola's taffeta hem rustled against the steps as she approached the door. She lifted her ebony skirts and winced. It had been three years since she had abandoned the trappings of mourning. She'd not expected to be wearing black again so soon. Donell had preferred her in blue - the colour of fresh water under a clear sky. She paused on the top step. He'd promised to take her to Venice before...

Viola tugged at the high collar. It was tighter than she remembered. She took a deep breath, letting the cool air spread into her lungs.

...before Anne abandoned her. Viola released her grip on her skirts and adjusted her tinted spectacles. This was a ruse; it wasn't real.

Her skirts swished as she turned to face number twenty-three Stanhope Street. Faint cracks lined the fading paint of the front door. Her smudged reflection drifted across the dull knocker. It was in dire need of a good spit and polish. Viola examined its face; the lion's head was loose, tilting slightly to the left. No wonder Professor Black was in need of more funds to fill the coffers. It seemed he preferred to spend money on inventions than on the upkeep of his house.

Viola glanced along the line of unkempt houses with bedraggled curtains or boarded up windows. The entire street seemed to need attention, making the Professor's house, and that of his two neighbours, seem almost stately. She raised her hand to the knocker.

The door opened.

A middle-aged footman with greying hair and watchful eyes stared back at her.

Viola lowered her hand. "I've an appointment to see Professor–"

"Good afternoon, Miss Marchland." He nodded and stepped aside. "Sir is expecting you."

Viola entered the hall.

"I am very early. I do hope I've not inconvenienced Professor Black?"

The footman clicked the door closed.

"Time is irrelevant."

He led the way along the hall, past a curiosity cabinet filled with exquisite oddities, past an ornately painted Oriental vase on the hall table, past the dining room. Crockery rattled as a maid cleared the table after luncheon. The footman continued to the end of the hall and halted in front of a closed door.

"Sir requested you join him in the laboratory."

The door squeaked open. A round-faced man with wiry mutton chop sideburns smiled; his narrow bow tie quivered as he nodded. "Welcome, Miss Marchland."

An antique grandfather clock clung to the wood-panelled wall near the doorway. The clunk of the pendulum measured each step as Viola followed the Professor into the dimly lit room. He paused at a podium facing the centre of the room and scanned its panel with its array of buttons and levers. He flicked a switch and raised his head to face the shadows engulfing the room, looking much like her old university anatomy lecturer readying to give a lecture.

Gas flames rose and flickered, banishing the shadows to the far corners of the room. A pavilion of burgundy velvet hung from a chain in the centre of the ceiling. Hidden gears whirred above her head. Chains clinked and rattled as the cloth jerked upwards, revealing a wooden platform hidden beneath.

The cloth inched higher. Metal glinted tantalisingly at its edge. The cloth twitched, swooped upwards and swivelled to one side. With a clunk, the chain disengaged and retracted into the roof. The velvet cloth slumped and crumpled onto the floor.

Flickering flames reflected off a gigantic Armillary Sphere; the contraption had several layers of concentric brass rings; at its heart sat an elaborately carved, mahogany chair upholstered in rich velvet - black as the starless night sky, absorbing the surrounding light. Its arms flattened out into equally elaborately-carved control panels, each with etched bronze and silver dials and displays. Leather straps lay folded neatly on the seat.

"The Chronosphere." Professor Black grinned.

Viola's eye widened. "It certainly looks impressive," she said. Like something she'd expect to read about in the science fantasies Sir Archibald had mentioned. What did he call it again?

Professor Black rolled a portable step up to the platform and clicked it into place. He dusted off his hands and lifted a section of metal that circumscribed the contraption, opening an entry to the sphere.

"Is there a specific question you wish to answer?" asked Professor Black.

"Pardon?" Viola glanced back at him.

"Most travellers have something they need to know." A smile flickered across Professor Black's lips. "Perhaps you want to peek at your Christmas presents?"

Viola's fingers twitched. Tempting, but she needed to help Sir Archibald first.

Professor Black returned to the control panel and waited.

What would a woman like Miss Marchland want? Viola straightened her shoulders. "When will women get the vote in England?" she asked.

"I'm sorry, that's beyond the Chronosphere's reach."

"Then take me as far as your contraption allows, Professor."

"There is a limit of three days' excursion."

Viola's shoulders drooped. Only three days? How would she discover the truth in such a short time?

"It's a matter of energy. We need more power to extend the range of travel," said Professor Black. "For that we need more funds."

Don't we all? Viola cleared her throat, remembering the ruse: sister and research partner of a wealthy scientist. She lifted her chin and raised an over-exaggerated eyebrow. "Then you had better impress me with this demonstration," she said.

"Three days it is." Professor Black clapped his hands together.

"I will miss Christmas dinner?" And Polly's plum pudding.

The Professor shook his head. "No need." He cranked back the dial and pressed a button. "Christmas dinner it is, then?"

"How does it work?" Viola climbed the step and grinned. Two Christmases!

She gathered her skirt, tugged it close and negotiated the exposed end of the metal ring, clicking the metal bar back in place to re-join the circle. She wiggled her bustle into the chair's soft velvet. It was exceedingly comfortable, considering it didn't cater for womens' fashion.

Professor Black motioned toward the straps. Viola nodded, pulled the straps over her chest and lap, and buckled them snugly.

"Please place your hands on the armrests, Miss Marchland."

Viola lowered her hands onto the polished mahogany. Her heart fluttered. Was she really going to do this? She examined the panels: two circular dials were embedded in the left arm. A vertical cog-like dial jutted out of the panel near a numerical tumbler, on the left. If she just reached out her finger...

"Does this control the destination?" she asked.

Professor Black nodded. "I will control the machine from here." He turned another dial.

The numbers spun on the tumbler and settled: 25. 12. 1889.

Viola stretched out a finger. "Can *I* control it from here?" She noted the order of dials as he manipulated the controls.

"Best not. I can't guarantee your safety outside the set parameters, Miss Marchland. We can't predict the future, but we can learn from it."

Viola's finger snapped away from the controls. She surveyed the contraption. From the inside it resembled a brass cage, not unlike a Faraday cage... Or a spherical Ascension Chamber. She'd nothing but bad experiences in such chambers. Her fingers trembled. *What was she doing?* The straps constricted her movement. Her heart raced.

"Are you sure you wish to proceed?" Professor Black's hand hovered over the large toggle on the panel. He grinned, one corner curling up a bit too much for her liking.

Viola squirmed, feeling not unlike a fox trapped in a snare. Her gaze traced the skeletal rings surrounding her. Sir Archibald needed her help. She couldn't abandon him now. And how could she pass up such an opportunity?

She nodded. *For Sir Archibald, and for science.*

"Very well, but be careful not to stray too far. You must not change your future. Meddling in the time stream could be hazardous to one's very existence." He grasped the toggle. "You cannot go back to mend your mistakes."

"Why not?" Viola narrowed her eyelid; they were almost Sir Archibald's own words.

"We don't know the toll each trip takes on the physiology," he replied. "As a woman of science, you must understand my caution. Until there is enough empirical evidence to the contrary, I am reluctant to allow others to take such risks."

The grandfather clock's tick echoed throughout the room. Viola held her breath. The dials on the chair's arms whirred. Numbers spun at a dizzying pace on the barrel. A two, then a five. *December*. The final numbers clicked into place: *1889*.

Professor Black flipped the toggle in the middle of the panel. The rings shook, lifted and spun, whooshing slowly at first, then picking up pace in varying directions, forming a barrier between the outside world and Viola.

The clock's tick hastened.

Tick. Tick.

Tick, tick.

The hands spun.

Tick, tick, tick.

Tick, tick, tick.

The minute hand blurred, each rotation completed in less than a second. The hour hand followed in its wake.

The gas light faded. Sparks crackled from the sphere. Viola's breaths quickened. The room spun. She closed her eye and gripped the chair, willing her stomach back down her throat.

The cacophonous whine of the rings steadied, until it mimicked the tick of the clock. Locks of hair danced across Viola's face, caught in clicking zephyrs: cool, rhythmic, hypnotising. Her fingers relaxed. She cracked open her eyelid.

A hum filled the room as the thwack of the rings slowed. The breeze waned. The wall sconces flickered and roared to life.

Viola peered at the grandfather clock. Its minute-hand whirred.

Tick, tick, tick, tick.

Tick, tick,

Tick.

The minute hand nudged the twelve and clicked into place.

Gong.

Seven o'clock. The last brass ring spun past her vision, and slid into place.

Blood thrummed in her ears. The room spiralled around her, in decreasing waves, and eased to a halt. Viola blinked, struggling to steady her focus. This must have been how Sir Archibald felt after his trip last night. No wonder he was so befuddled.

The laboratory door opened. Professor Black stepped into the room. He straightened his cravat, tapped his pocket watch and slipped it into his waistcoat pocket.

"Merry Christmas, Miss Marchland. I do hope you like roast turkey."

Greenery filled the room, draping the paintings and lining the window. Bright red holly berries dotted the boughs. Miniature candles twinkled on the tips of the Christmas tree's branches. Hand-made cards dangled from string and skimmed the bottom of the mantelpiece. The fire crackled, its flames danced in the hearth, ebbing and flowing with the buzz of jolly conversation.

Professor Black had invited his sister, Phillipa Whitehead, and her husband to the dinner party. Mrs Whitehead had an air of an elegant woman forced to cope in trying circumstances: her impeccably-tailored midnight blue velvet gown glowed under the gaslight; green flashing eyes assessed her dinner companions and found herself in need of entertainment. Her crown of red curls bounced as she snatched up a Christmas cracker, thrust it in the direction of Mr Whitehead and giggled.

Mr Whitehead sighed and grabbed the paper.

"Now pull!" Mrs Whitehead jerked the cylindrical parcel toward her. Paper ripped and trinkets spilled onto the white tablecloth.

Viola peered through the silver-plated table candelabra and sipped more wine.

The feast was magnificent: roast turkey with cranberry sauce, steaming French potatoes, Brussels sprouts and honeyed peas. A dish of pork pies sat on one end of the table. The smell of cinnamon pervaded everything, though Viola could not place its source.

Mr Whitehead returned to chasing wayward peas around his plate. He sighed, flipped his fork and scooped a dollop of cranberry sauce onto a slice of turkey.

"Will you be attending the Royal Society's New Year's Eve Party, Miss Marchland?" asked Professor Black.

Voila shook her head and frowned. All this talk of parties! It was getting late and she was running out of time to find something to help Sir Archibald.

Professor Black's smile slipped. He placed his glass between strategically placed bowers of ivy. "I must apologise. Here we are talking of parties, when you, dear lady, are still in mourning."

Viola gulped down her mouthful of wine and lowered her gaze. Her black sleeves contrasted with the stark white of the tablecloth. She had forgotten her ruse. She must remember to play the part if she was to save Sir Archibald.

Phillipa Whitehead coughed mid-giggle. A Brussels sprout fell from her fork and plopped onto her plate.

"Oh, dear," Mrs Whitehead whispered. She silently placed her cutlery on the table.

Viola shifted in her seat. A change of subject was required.

"You are fortunate to find residence so close to King's College. But does the noise of the Chronosphere prove bothersome to the neighbours?"

"This was my father's house," replied Professor Black. "He owned it when the Royal Society of Science was still at King's. I acquired the buildings either side of the house some years ago before the houses nearby were vacated." Professor Black poured another glass of wine. "There are rumours of grand plans for expanding the College. Perhaps they will require more research assistants, Miss Marchland?"

"You're a scientist?" Mrs Whitehead scooped up the Brussels

sprout. "I must admit I am lost when my brother tries to explain his latest..." She waved her hand in the air. "... Whatsit."

Mr Whitehead desisted from torturing his meal.

Viola pulled a handkerchief from her purse and eyed him as she dabbed her eye theatrically. "I was my brother's research assistant. The day of the accident..." She sniffed. "I was injured in the fulmination."

"Your tinted spectacles? Are they—?" Mrs Whitehead gasped.

"My eyes never fully recovered. I cannot abide any significant light source." Viola folded her handkerchief, placed it in her lap and nodded. "I am fated to live in the shadows and forever view the world through obsidian-coloured lenses."

All three guests stared at her with open mouths.

Viola bit her lip. Perhaps that was too much? She shifted in her chair. "I promised dear Albert I would honour his wishes to fund your chronological research."

Professor Black smiled. "I'm glad he deemed the Chronosphere worthy of consideration," he said.

Viola relaxed. They believed her.

"But I will require empirical evidence. Infallible proof." She twisted the corner of her handkerchief. "For the lawyers, you understand?"

Mr Whitehead glanced at Professor Black and sipped his wine.

"Of course," said Professor Black. "Something our earlier selves would not know?"

"That would suffice." Viola turned her wine glass and stared into the liquid. A patch of red light splashed across the cloth, bounced off the silver candelabra and flitted across the window. "Perhaps the big news of the day? Something that happened Christmas Eve? I require to finalise any endowment with the bank before I return to Europe tomorrow afternoon. I shan't be returning before Easter."

"Knowledge of the future is dangerous." Professor Black straightened the knife beside his plate.

Viola surveyed her dinner companions. She wouldn't find out anything here. She needed to get out of the house.

"However, I can say this," he said. "You first met my dear sister when you left, on your return to your original time."

"A boy ran out in front of my carriage," said Mrs Whitehead. "I still have the bruises!"

"I do hope he wasn't hurt?" asked Viola.

Professor Black placed his hand on his sister's elbow. "Only time will tell," he replied.

The butler's footsteps rang along the hallway. He wheeled a food trolley into the dining room and placed a platter of mince pies and a dish of Nesselrode pudding on the table, before retreating to the shadows.

"Nesselrode pudding," Mrs Whitehead clapped her hands. "My favourite."

Viola stared at the pudding. Her heart sank. The evening was almost finished; she was missing Christmas dinner with Henry and Sir Archibald will be... She swallowed. What was the point of a second Christmas if it wasn't spent with her friends?

Mrs Whitehead's hands fell onto the table. "You've gone pale, Miss Marshland. Are you unwell?"

Viola managed a faint smile. She mustn't forget the part she was playing - for Sir Archibald, and the Empire. She retrieved the handkerchief and sniffed. Watch yourself, Viola. Don't overdo it. *You'll give yourself away.* "Nesselrode pudding was Albert's favourite as well," she said.

Mrs Whitehead leaned closer and took Viola's hand. "There,

there, my dear. A hot cup of tea will make you feel better."

Professor Black motioned to the butler. He emerged from the shadows, nodded and left the dining room.

Viola glanced at the clock. Almost midnight. Five hours and I've discovered nothing. Some detective she was! If she could contact Polly, find out if she has discovered anything over the past few days?

"Would it be safe to venture outside?" she asked. "I would dearly like to visit my friends. They will be so disappointed if they discovered I was still in London for Christmas, and didn't visit. I would only be an hour or two, and I promise not to mention the Chronosphere."

Mrs Whitehead folded her napkin and placed it on the table.

"That is the advantage of time travel, Miss Marshland." Professor Black leaned back in his chair. "When you return all will be as if this never happened. Time will continue on its original course. Only you shall remember this version, unless of course you decide to dine with us for Christmas again."

Viola's eye widened. "So time can be changed?" she asked. "But, if as you say, they won't remember any of this when I return to my original time, then what is the harm in visiting my friends?"

"The future is still unlived, Miss Marshland."

The butler returned and poured Viola a cup of tea. She picked up the tea cup and eyed Professor Black over the rim. Perhaps there was a way to gain more time, to find an answer to Sir Archibald's conundrum? She needed more time.

"And the past? Can it be relived?" she asked.

Professor Black straightened in his chair. Mrs Whitehead's cup rattled on its saucer.

"Can your machine travel back in time? I was wondering, no hoping, there was some possibility...?" She sniffed and caught her breath. Not too over-dramatic this time? "Perhaps I could return to the day of my brother's accident?"

"One can never go back," replied Professor Black

"Why not?" Viola lifted the cup to her lips and breathed in its warm vapour. It was sweet, with a hint of cinnamon and fruit.

"It's not safe." He waved away the tea pot and held up his wine glass. Mrs Whitehead followed suit.

"Travelling is too unpredictable." The butler filled his glass with wine. "Going forward we can glimpse what may, or may not, happen and there is less danger in corrupting one's future, as it has not yet arrived."

"But it has," said Viola.

"Has what?" asked Mrs Whitehead.

"The future is happening now," replied Viola.

Professor Black's tea cup remained untouched. Why was no one drinking their tea? She lowered her cup. She'd run afoul of a supposed innocent cup of tea before. She sniffed the vapour again. She could taste the sweetness.

"What if you triggered an accident that killed your mother?" asked Professor Black. He gulped the dregs of his wine. "Would you cease to exist?"

"If one changed the past, even in the smallest degree, who is to say what the consequences would be?" He picked up his tea cup and took a swig.

Viola held her breath and waited. Nothing happened.

"All this talk of time travel is making my head ache." Mrs Whitehead sighed.

Viola let her breath escape slowly. Her shoulders relaxed. *You're getting paranoid, Viola Stewart.* She raised her cup and took a sip. A fine mix of Darjeeling and Assam, with a hint of cinnamon and apple. "It tastes like apple cider."

"Clever, isn't it?" said Mrs Whitehead. "It's a special Christmas brew."

The clock chimed midnight.

"Time we get you back, Miss Marshland," said Professor Black.

Chapter Two

Propositions

The door to number twenty-three Stanhope Street clicked shut. Viola's ears still hummed from the aftereffects of returning to her original time. She pulled on her kid gloves and huffed. Nothing. She'd learned nothing. Her trip to the future had proved decidedly uninformative. But what had she expected? Answers never come that easy.

She glared back at the house. Sir Archibald was relying on her. His life depended on it, and she'd wasted her chance. She couldn't leave him to such an ignominious fate. Treason, indeed! Sir Archibald would never betray Queen nor country.

A chill breeze swirled around her, sending a shiver down her back. She pulled her *visite* tight and glanced across the street. A golden rim of fading sunlight edged the roofs of the vacant dwellings. Viola squinted to examine them. The lower windows were shuttered. Heavy curtains clothed those on the upper levels - a perfect vantage point to wait, and watch, until the household went to bed.

Only one trip? Ha! No matter the risk, she had to make another journey in that infernal machine. She'd studied the Professor. The procedure appeared simple enough: dial in the date, set the time. The Professor and his colleague had an engagement on New Year's Eve; that would provide a few hours to gather more information.

Professor Black's caution tugged at her memory: *You must not influence your future. You cannot go back to mend your mistakes.*

But what if she could? If there wasn't enough time while the Professor was at his party, she could continue her investigation on her return. Any other information, gleaned between now and New Year, could be delivered to her in the future. She *could* change Sir Archibald's fate.

Viola's head spun. Was it the contemplation of time travel, or the remnants of the return voyage? She took a deep breath. She'd have to tell Polly to deliver the information to her here on New Year's Eve.

How clever. Viola grinned. She would have two chances to investigate and can bring back the information with her - and prevent not only Sir Archibald's untimely demise but prove he is not a traitor.

Wheels clattered at the end of the street, reminding her of the noise of the Chronosphere. Viola paused on the steps. Her shoulders slumped. The machine would wake the house. They'd discover she'd used the machine and be waiting for her to return. How would she explain her intrusion?

Viola's mind raced; there had to be a solution. She just needed to apply some logic: Sir Archibald had said no one was home when he visited yesterday evening. They wouldn't be waiting for her, if she returned before she arrived. Perfect. She skipped down the steps.

The carriage rattled closer. Viola struggled to focus on the movement. Its black hulk blurred. The world lurched. Her stomach churned as she grabbed for the stone balustrade. Perhaps she'd not yet recovered from the effects of travelling?

A shadow flitted in the corner of her eye, moving toward the carriage. Viola blinked to clear her vision. A young boy darted across the street. Viola gripped the balustrade. "Watch out!"

The horse reared. The carriage shuddered.

The boy cursed as he skidded on the cobblestones and dashed into an alley.

"Steady. Steady." The driver jerked the reins tight. He twisted back toward the carriage. "Are you all right, Miss?"

"Are we there?" The voice was familiar.

The cab door opened. A woman in emerald velvet, her fiery hair almost hidden under an ornate hat, stepped out of the carriage and swirled up the steps. It was Professor Black's sister.

"I'm bruised head to toe." Mrs Whitehead glared at the driver. "Move along. You'll get nothing from me."

The driver's whip cracked above the horse's head. He grumbled and sped the cab off into the growing shadows.

"Are you all right, Mrs Whitehead?" asked Viola.

"Fine, thank you." Mrs Whitehead peered at Viola. "Have we met?"

Viola shook her head. Not yet. "I'm... Miss Marchland," she replied. "I believe your brother is expecting you."

Viola descended the steps and adjusted her tinted spectacles so she could spy Mrs Whitehead's reflection in the side mirror as she bustled through the front door.

Long shadows swathed the street. Small bursts of light erupted in the distance; the lamplighters were on their way.

Viola slipped into a narrow alley, between the buildings across the road, and made her way toward the servants' entrance. The back gate was unlatched. Viola slipped through the gate and eased the latch home.

The yard was pitch black, hidden in the shadow of the high fence, with no moon to cast useful light. Viola lifted the left tinted lens of her spectacles. It made little difference. If only she'd brought her night goggles. She felt her way along the wooden fence, and along the wall of the house until she found a door.

Viola lifted the silver locket from her neck, plucked out two of its amethyst-headed lock picks and searched out the keyhole. The door swung open. Not locked? Viola raised an eyebrow and entered.

The room was even darker than outside. Viola edged along the wall, her fingers feeling for any hint of where she was. She reached out into the darkness and groped the air.

Anything.

Her foot slammed into metal. A loud rattle skidded across the hard floor. She winced. A coal scuttle? If this was the kitchen, perhaps there's...

She shuffled forward, searching the room with her hands. Her nails scraped on wood. A bench? She wiped her hand along its surface. A cold metal object barred the way. She felt its shape. A lantern. Liquid sloshed. Viola smiled. She edged her hand along the edge, found a drawer and pulled it open. A faint smell of sulphur tugged at her nostrils. She struck a match. At last, some light.

The kitchen was small and bare. Flecks of rust peppered the dusty stove. A cracked jug sat on the bench. A coal scuttle lay by the opposite wall, near a discarded poker.

There was a muffled thump on the ceiling above. Viola held her breath, dimmed the lantern and cocked her ear toward the sound. Another faint knock, this time near the front of the house. Was someone upstairs?

She commandeered the poker and tiptoed toward the servants' steps. They were narrow, claustrophobic and in dire need of a good scrub.

The door at the top of the stairs opened out into a hallway. A faint light flickered through the front window at the far end, casting a glow onto the ceiling. The house was silent.

Viola stepped into the hall. The light faded. She crept along the hall toward the front room. The door was open and the curtains drawn. A horizontal shadow pierced the curtains. Viola tweaked the knob on the lantern.

The light reflected off a bronze telescope near the window. Its end peeked through a gap in the curtain. An armchair sat next to its supporting frame. A heavily-padded leather sofa faced the window, several feet away. An octagonal side table stood near the door.

Viola placed the lantern on the table and thrust out the poker in defence.

A faint aroma of fresh, spiced leather wafted in the air. A familiar, comforting smell. Viola closed her eye and drew a deep breath.

Henry? Her eye snapped open.

"Henry Collins, you should be convalescing. How dare you–?"

A warm hand clasped over her mouth.

Viola raised the poker. A firm grip stayed her hand.

"Do be quiet. The point of surveillance is not to let the subject know you are doing so." The voice was calm and concise, and one she'd heard before in the dark.

"That's impossible," she mumbled, as she turned her head slowly; bare skin brushed against her cheek. The poker twisted from her grip.

"Only improbable."

She glimpsed a well-tailored waistcoat, shirtsleeves rolled up to reveal athletic forearms. Metal glinted on her assailant's chest.

"Mr Wood?" The hand fell from her mouth. "You're a long way from Scotland," she said.

"Not 'Wood'." He ran his hand over his moustache.

"So, it is Mr Peabody?" Viola rubbed her wrist.

He dropped the poker near the empty fireplace and shook his head.

"Then what shall I call you?"

"Chester." He kissed her hand. "Mr Chester, at your service."

His hair smelled of new leather and spices. Viola's heart fluttered; her gaze followed him to the window.

"I must say you are looking... less bedraggled than last we met, Doctor Stewart." He sat on the armchair and realigned the telescope. "Though black does not become you."

Viola peeked through the curtain; the telescope was trained at Professor Black's house.

"I hear congratulations are in order." Mr Chester straightened his waistcoat. "Though I hadn't thought his injuries were that serious."

Viola snatched her hand away from the curtain. "How did you know Doctor Collins was injured?" she asked.

Mr Chester peered through the telescope.

"You had me at a disadvantage in Scotland," he said. "I had been under the impression you were... unattached. Had I known, I would have behaved in a more appropriate manner."

Warmth spread up Viola's cheeks. Why hadn't she mentioned Henry? And why was she here, with a strange man? Unchaperoned. *At night*! Her fingers twitched. What would Lady Calthorpe think of her? Viola held her breath and stepped away from the window. She needed to concentrate.

"When is the happy day?" asked Mr Chester.

Viola retreated into the shadows. She just couldn't... How could she...? When Anne could be... She swallowed, not brave enough to say the word.

"We haven't set a date yet." Viola's thumb flicked at her engagement ring.

"I see." Mr Chester refocused the telescope and peered through the lens. "Have you ever considered a different vocation, Doctor Stewart? We need someone we can trust. The Department of Curiosities offers a life of independent adventure; no one following you, to keep an eye on you." He ran his fingers over his moustache.

"No one?" Viola edged back toward the window. Rivulets of rain smeared the glass.

"Of course, you would be bound by the Secrets Act. You could tell no one. Not even your fiancé."

Not tell Henry? Her heart thickened in her chest.

"But it would open avenues to pursue other investigations without hindrance," he continued.

Anne? Viola's eye widened. Could she finally discover her sister's fate? She moved another step closer. The smell of spiced leather tugged at her senses, clouding her thoughts, reminding her of Henry. Her shoulders relaxed. *She could be free to move on.*

Mr Chester turned away from the telescope. One corner of his lip curled.

Viola paused and crossed her arms. Had that been his intended design all along? To entice her into joining his precious Department? She peered through the window. Or was he trying to distract her from something else?

"Tell me, Mr Chester, if that is indeed your name," said Viola, "do you get lonely?"

Mr Chester remained silent.

"Is that why you attempt to entice me away from my fiancé, with the promise of liberty and emancipation?"

"Ah, the point of a secret department is for it to remain secret. No exceptions. A small price to pay for independence in a man's world, wouldn't you agree?"

Viola twisted the ring on her finger. She loved Henry. "But why should I, when I have both?"

Mr Chester, cleared his throat and turned his attention back to the telescope. Viola smiled and eyed the sofa behind them. A greatcoat lay crumpled on one end.

"I assume you are in London on a Department matter, Mr Chester?" she asked. It was time for him to share *his* secrets. Viola moved the coat aside, sat on the sofa and rearranged her skirts. She could play these games as well as he. "Or are you following me?" she asked.

Mr Chester shook his head. His chair squeaked on the floorboards as he rose.

"Just a pleasant coincidence." He sat down on the couch beside Viola. His dark hair fell over one eye.

Viola straightened the ring on her finger and smiled. She was onto his tricks. She'd not be distracted again. "May I enquire as to your interest in Professor Black?"

Mr Chester remained silent.

"Or shall I be required to sign more papers before you can answer that?"

"No need," he replied. "Remember our adventure in Scotland?"

"The smugglers?" She still had an adorable mechanical Bot as a souvenir. Viola bit her cheek, trying not to smile.

He nodded.

"I followed their trail here. Professor Black's storehouse is stocked with ill-gotten gains." He leaned back in his chair. "Your turn, Doctor Stewart. What brings you to Stanhope Street?"

"I'm..." It was now his turn to remain uninformed; she would not make it easy for him. "Helping a friend."

"Yes." He glanced in Viola's direction. "Tell me more about Sir Archibald Huntington-Smythe."

Viola caught her breath. "How did you–?"

"Come now, Doctor Stewart. I've read your dossier, remember. Friend or not, he has been associating with individuals of dubious standing."

Viola jumped to her feet. *Never!*

"Sir Archibald's reputation is beyond reproach. He would never..." She crossed over to the telescope and stared out of the window. Only one light remained burning in Professor Black's house.

"But is he trustworthy?" asked Mr Chester.

"I trust him with my life," she replied.

"Nevertheless, I need to know how he is involved, Doctor Stewart. There are plans in motion. And I have been sent to prevent them."

Ah, there it was. Viola spun on her heel. "So, all this has been to gain my trust, so you can extract information on Sir

Archibald?"

"He has a privileged position as personal physician to the Queen. If he was to use that position, or was coerced into doing so..." Mr Chester pinched his lip between steepled his fingers. "There would be serious ramifications, not just for your friend, but for the Empire." He stared at her over the top of his hands. "So, I ask you again, Doctor Stewart, tell me how Sir Archibald is involved in all this."

"Professor Black is petitioning for funds to expand his research."

"No blackmail?" he asked.

Viola's heart sank into her stomach. Was Professor Black planning to blackmail Sir Archibald? "It's not what you think," she replied.

"No?"

"No." Viola clenched her fists. She spoke quickly: "Sir Archibald has implored me to find the truth. He would *never* give in to blackmail."

"You are a loyal friend, Doctor Stewart, but I–"

"No, listen." She strode toward him. "Sir Archibald dies tomorrow."

Mr Chester's hands fell onto his lap.

"They have a time machine. I think they plan to–"

Mr Chester stood slowly.

"They have what?" The colour drained from his face.

Viola raised an eyebrow. She'd never seen him rattled before.

"Then it is true?" His voice cracked. He moved toward the window, each step slow and deliberate, and sat in the chair next to the telescope.

"Yes, I've seen it," she replied.

"And it works?" He pressed his eyes against the telescope's

eyepiece.

"It appears so." Viola straightened her shoulders. "I had Christmas dinner with Professor Black and his sister in two days' time."

Mr Chester sat in silence, staring at the house for several seconds; there was no witty retort, no flashing smile. He sniffed, unhooked the telescope and collapsed the tube with a snap, and turned to face Viola.

"The Department thanks you for your co-operation, Doctor Stewart. I commend your loyalty to Sir Archibald." His moustache twitched. "And to your fiancé." He placed the telescope in a velvet-lined box. "But I have a duty to a higher authority. Sir Archibald must be detained for further questioning and the machine will be confiscated."

"No! I need that machine. I need to prove his innocence." Viola grabbed Mr Chester's arm. "Just give me one more day."

He flipped the latch on the box closed. "Very well. I will allow Sir Archibald one more day. But if you warn him, you will be committing treason." The gleam returned to his eyes. "And your fiancé will not be pleased."

Viola released the grip on his arm. "I can make my own decisions, Mr Chester. I don't need anyone's approval. Not Henry's, and certainly not yours."

"I can see why Doctor Collins admires you." He bowed his head. "I will escort you home." He retrieved his greatcoat, placed it on Viola's shoulders and gestured in the direction of the door. "But you are not to enter Professor Black's house. That machine is now under Department jurisdiction."

"But, you just said–"

"I must insist, Doctor Stewart. You don't realise the danger you have courted. Professor Black has dangerous allies."

"Then how shall I prove Sir Archibald's innocence?"

"I will complete the investigation," replied Mr Chester.

"Do I have a choice?"

"No. You must trust me, Doctor Stewart."

Rain tapped on the window, obscuring the street. Viola slipped her arms into the sleeves of Mr Chester's coat and pulled it tight.

"You must earn it, Mr Chester."

Flames licked the fireplace. A blackened chunk of wood shifted, fell to the floor of the hearth and crumbled into charred fragments. A shiver flitted down Archibald's neck. He puffed on his pipe; his gaze tracked its smoke as it swirled toward the fireplace and mingled with the flames.

Viola had been gone too long. He should have handled this himself.

The parlour door swung open. Polly entered, settled a food tray on the side table, and started to light the gas wall sconces. A warm glow filled the room.

He glanced at the clock on the mantelpiece. Almost eight o'clock.

"Any news?" he asked.

Polly poked the fire. "Sir, I'm worried," she whispered.

Archibald shook his head and returned his attention to the dying fire. Henry would never forgive him if anything had happened to Viola.

Hooves clopped on the cobblestones outside. A carriage rattled to a stop. Archibald twisted in his chair. Rain pounded on the darkened windows.

"At last." He sucked on his pipe. Smoke filled his lungs; his body relaxed.

There was a tap on the front door. Polly smiled and skipped from the room. Footsteps echoed in the hall.

Polly hurried through the door, twisting the corner of her apron.

"It's about time." Archibald jumped to his feet and spun to face the doorway.

"Doctor Collins to see Miss Viola." She took Henry's coat, stepped aside and shook off the droplets of rain.

Henry leaned heavily on an ornate walking stick. A mechanical splint supported his left leg. His face was pale, his waistcoat crooked, his jacket dishevelled. He hobbled toward the fireplace and collapsed into the chair facing Archibald.

Archibald lowered himself back into his chair and tucked his pipe under the edge of the supper tray.

"You should be resting," said Archibald. "You could end up with a permanent limp. Or worse..." He glared at Henry through narrowed eyelids. "You could require my more advanced mechanical services."

Curls of pipe smoke escaped from under the tray. Henry raised his eyes and looked Archibald in the eye. "You said you'd give up that vile habit," said Henry.

Archibald waved away stray wisps of smoke and straightened his spectacles. Polly hovered near the doorway, avoiding Henry's gaze.

"Viola missed tea this afternoon," said Henry.

Archibald and Polly exchanged glances.

"Come on, Archie. I may have injured my leg, but my mental faculties are intact. What has Viola gotten herself into?"

Archibald's fingers twitched toward his pipe. Henry's moustache twitched. "Where is your Mistress?" he asked Polly.

Polly straightened her apron and bit her lip.

"It's not the girl's fault, Henry."

"Tell me what is going on, Archie!" Henry gripped his cane and stomped it on the floor.

Archibald took a deep breath and steadied his hands. "Viola makes her own decisions," he said.

Henry leaned closer. "If anything has happened to her..." His moustache drooped.

"Viola is an intelligent woman and quite capable of looking after herself."

Henry slumped back into his chair. "But does the world know that?"

Rivulets of water rolled down Viola's neck. She flipped up the collar of her borrowed coat and dashed to her front door, turning only briefly to watch the carriage trundle off around the corner into High Street.

Light flooded out of the open door and spilled onto the porch. She dashed up the steps.

Polly stood in the doorway and curtsied. "Doctor Collins is here to see you, Miss."

Viola glanced into the hall. Sir Archibald hovered behind Polly, fidgeting with his spectacles. Henry hobbled from the parlour to join him, one leg encased in a jumble of whirring gears and pistons attached to a metal leg brace.

"Hello, Vi." He shifted his weight onto his walking cane and frowned.

"Henry Collins! You should be–"

"You're wet," replied Henry.

Polly closed the door behind Viola and stared at the floor.

Water dripped from lank curls of hair and seeped under Viola's bodice. Drops ran off the cuffs of the greatcoat and collected on her fingertips. She flicked them to the ground. Drenched skirts clung to her calves. She shivered and glanced at her feet and the ever-expanding puddle of water that collected there.

Polly took the greatcoat and examined it as she hung it on the hallstand. Henry's gaze followed the coat.

"New coat?" asked Henry. His mechanical brace clicked as he shifted his weight. "Sir Archibald was just about to tell me about his afternoon."

Polly glanced at Viola, then at Henry and cleared her throat. "I'll fetch some towels."

Henry waited until Polly had left the hall and turned to Sir Archibald. "Weren't you, Archie?"

"The jig is up, I'm afraid, old girl." Sir Archibald sighed and shoved his hands into his jacket pockets.

Viola stepped forward; one foot sploshed in the water.

"It's a matter of life and death," said Viola. "You are injured. We had no choice. Sir Archibald dies tomorrow. Professor Black wouldn't allow him to travel a second time."

"Travel where?" asked Henry.

"When," whispered Sir Archibald.

"What?" Henry raised an eyebrow. "Did you say: *Archie dies?* How could you possibly know that?"

"I travelled through time, Henry!" Viola grinned.

"You what? Time travel isn't possible." Henry turned to face Sir Archibald. "What is going on, Archie?"

"Sir Archibald will die tomorrow, and I travelled forward in time to find out how to prevent it." Viola wiped her hand on her bodice and placed it on Henry's.

Henry shook his head.

"Show him, Sir Archibald," said Viola.

Sir Archibald retrieved the crumpled newspaper from his jacket pocked, flicked it open and handed it to Henry.

Henry read the headline, dropped the newspaper on hall table and leaned on his cane.

"Is this true? That scientist at the Meeting? He was serious?"

Sir Archibald nodded. "We've both travelled, Henry."

"I had Christmas dinner with the Professor," said Viola. "It's all true. We can't let Sir Archibald die. I have to return. To save him."

"And Sir Archibald thought it prudent for you to go alone?" asked Henry. "I won't have it, Vi. It's too dangerous."

"You won't–?" Viola's heart froze. She released Henry's hand. "You don't own me, Henry Collins. You don't get to tell me what I can or can't do. Not now." Her thumb clicked on her engagement ring. "Not ever."

Viola's foot slapped in the puddle. Drips quivered off the hem of her skirt and plopped onto her boots, seeping under the laces.

Polly scurried in with a bundle of towels in her arms. She presented one to Viola and bent down to mop up the floor.

Viola examined the towels as Polly soaked up the water. She ran her toe through the puddle beneath her and eyed Mr Chester's coat on the hall stand. It hung, in a heavy, sopping mass, next to Sir Archibald's dry coat. Bone dry. How had he managed to keep dry? *It will be raining on Christmas day.*

"Sir Archibald, you had Christmas dinner with Professor Black?" she asked.

"Roast beef and Brussels sprouts." He licked his lips.

"Did it rain when you found the paperboy outside, in the

street?"

"No, it was a glorious night. Not a cloud in the sky."

No rain? Perhaps the future had been altered? Had Sir Archibald's interaction with the paperboy generated a new temporal crossover and broken down the logic of causality? The Professor had warned her of the possibility. But how? She had heeded their warnings and not left the house. She leaned on the hall table. And how could that possibly affect the weather?

"It rained when I had Christmas dinner," she whispered. "No, something isn't right."

"Viola?" Henry stepped forward. Deep lines etched his forehead. "Polly, fetch your Mistress a warm blanket."

Viola's eye widened; she stepped back.

"It wasn't raining." She shoved the towel into Henry's hands. "Don't you see? I have to go back." She wrenched open the hall table drawer and snatched up her gilded pistol and night goggles.

"But–?" His moustache drooped.

Viola stared into Henry's bright blue eyes. Fine wrinkles had formed at the corners.

"Trust me, Henry." She grabbed a coat and dashed out into the street in search of a Brougham cab.

Chapter Three

A Chronic Disaster

iola held her breath and felt for the floor in the dark with her toe. It touched solid ground. She let out her breath and pulled her skirts free of the windowsill, her boot snagging in a snarl of silk. She lost her balance, tumbled into the room and rolled headfirst into a piece of unseen furniture, with a thud. A faint rip made her wince.

Distant lamp light outlined an opening on the other side of the room. Voices wafted through the doorway.

"But you promised!" It was Professor Black. His voice was muffled.

Viola ducked behind the unidentified furniture.

"You said if I delivered the surgeon–," he hissed.

"You have not completed your side of the bargain." A woman's voice. Viola strained to hear.

The light receded. Viola waited, until the only noise she could hear was her own breathing. She flipped up the ruching of her bustle skirt, and reached into the pocket concealed under her bustle to retrieve her night goggles and slipped them on over her eye patch. Large, dark shapes filled the room. She clicked an auxiliary lens into position. Shadowy outlines of chairs and sofas resolved out of the dark. This must be the parlour.

Viola picked her way through the room toward the hall. Professor Black and his conspirator were nowhere to be seen. She hugged the wall and made her way along the hall until she found a door. She tested the knob. The door clicked open.

The room was dark. She placed her ear against the crack and listened. All was silent. She took a deep breath, slipped inside and scanned the room. Large square shapes lined the walls. A low, rectangular outline suggested a desk on the far side. Behind it was a smaller, paler square area on the wall.

Viola inched her way forward, feeling her way. She glanced over the desk: a blotter, pen and ink, a pile of letters, textbooks. A pile of notes sat on one end, next to an etched metal casket. She moved the desk chair out of the way, careful not to make a noise.

A portrait of a serene blonde woman beckoned Viola closer. She turned her attention to the intriguing area hidden on the wall behind it, unhooked the portrait and propped it against the desk. A fine crack outlined a two-foot square area of one of the wooden panels. She tapped on the wall. It sounded hollow. A hidden cupboard? A safe?

Viola clicked another lens in front of her goggles and ran her fingers over the panel. A slight recess marked the keyhole. She extracted two amethyst-headed lock picks from the silver locket around her neck. There was a satisfying click. She slipped the lock picks home.

Gears whirred in the wall. The wall panel slid open to reveal a wall safe. Viola peeked into the void. What could be so important?

Inside was a mahogany box, approximately one foot square, assorted loose papers and several document pouches. Viola caught her breath. This could be what she was looking for! Perhaps risking another journey to the future wasn't necessary after all?

She eased the box out of the safe and placed it on the desk, then retrieved a pouch and unwound the cord securing it shut. She flipped through the contents. It was a dossier.

Viola's heart raced. She grabbed the remaining document pouches, five in all. She opened another pouch, and another. The fourth was a dossier on Professor Marchland. Large capital letters were printed across the front page in a steady, confident hand:

EXTINGUISHED: FILE CLOSED/COMPLETE

Dead? Was Professor Black behind Professor Marchland's death? She closed the pouch. Was there a dossier on Sir Archibald? Viola swallowed and picked up the final folder. Her fingers trembled as she unwound the cord, slipped out the pages and read the handwritten notation on the front page:

IN PROGRESS.

She turned the page:

SIR ARCHIBALD HUNTINGTON-SMYTHE

Her heart sank. Poor Archie. She skimmed the pages, straining to read the notes, even with the augmented vision of her goggles. There were pages of personal information, a listing of his daily routine and detailed information of his access to the Queen. There was even a list of his favourite foods.

One page had a report on Professor Black's lecture at the Research Meeting. Another detailed his plot to gain Sir Archibald's confidence and a plan to persuade him to travel forward to Christmas day. There was even mention of Sir Archibald's procurement of the newspaper. Viola gasped. The Professor knew he had it!

In the margin was a scribbled notation:

This is an opportune moment to act, as subject's friend, Police Surgeon Doctor Henry Collins, is unable to assist due to a recent injury. This will reduce possible support or assistance during the operation and increase subject's isolation.

Viola shoved the pages back into the pouch and wrapped the cord around it. She snatched up Professor Marchland's dossier and paused. She eyed the box. What else could the Professor be hiding? She flipped the brass latch and eased open the lid.

A lifeless wax mask stared back at her. Viola's eyes widened. It was Sir Archibald! She'd seen similar craftsmanship before: a wax mask of Arthur Doyle made by an ex-employee of Madame Tussaud's - part of a foiled plot by the Men in Grey. Viola slumped into the chair. Was Professor Black involved in one of their plots? What had Sir Archibald stumbled into?

Voices drifted down the hall into the room. She slapped the lid shut and tucked the box under her arm. The voices grew louder.

"You got rid of him." Professor Black was returning.

Viola shoved the remaining pouches back into the wall safe.

"No matter, Marchland brought us Sir Archibald - before he had a change of heart, before he couldn't stomach the idea of betrayal." This time the woman's voice was clear.

Viola's heart jumped into her throat. It was Mrs Whitehead. She hadn't seemed the leader type.

"But you removed him before he could give us the money," whined the Professor. "I can't finish my research without it."

"You'll get your money from his estate. The sister doesn't suspect a thing. Just make sure she doesn't find you when it's all done."

"I can't wait that long. You must pay me what you promised now."

The footsteps paused. They were close. Viola's heart thumped as she strained to hear.

"You haven't completed your end of the bargain," said Mrs Whitehead. "I need the surgeon's agreement. You will not get your payment until he provides us with the information we need when he returns. This time make sure you give him enough of that drug."

"Will the mask be convincing?"

"Just keep him out of the way until the task is complete. He must take the blame. I'll be leaving as soon as this farce is over."

Viola's heart froze. So they are behind the assassination attempt and intend to blame it all on Sir Archibald. She tugged on the safe door. Cogs whirred; the lock clicked. The footsteps quickened.

Viola glanced at the wall portrait leaning against the desk and frowned. There was no time to replace it. She snatched up the two pouches and ducked under the desk.

The door creaked. The desk's shadow flowed up the wall as their lamp moved closer. Gas hissed. Viola tucked herself further under the desk to avoid the light. Footsteps crossed the room. Closer. Closer. Viola held her breath.

"But what if he doesn't return tomorrow?" asked Professor Black, his voice clear.

"Make sure he does, and that he does not leave here. That is what you are being paid for. My job is to ensure the Fat Empress is eliminated. We must have control over–"

The footsteps stopped.

"Check the files," hissed Mrs Whitehead.

Footsteps hurried to the wall. The door whirred open.

Viola reached into her pocket for her pistol. She had two shots. At this close range, it should be enough. Her fingers trembled. She'd rather not–

He gasped. "The box is *gone*."

"We need that box!" Mrs Whitehead's boots clicked across the room.

Viola peeked out from under the desk. Professor Black was only a few feet away. He turned to face Mrs Whitehead, his face twisted in fear.

"It's not my– " He paused, directing his attention toward the desk. He took a step closer.

Viola let out a slow, controlled breath.

His grip on her arm was stronger than she expected. He yanked her clear of the desk. Viola's boots scraped on the floor as she struggled to break free. Her pistol jerked out of her hand and skittered along the wooden floor.

Professor Black dragged her onto the chair.

The box clattered onto the floor. Viola clutched the pouches; she couldn't lose proof of Sir Archibald's innocence. She bowed her head, her hair falling over her face, and stared at the box. She needed its contents to prove their plan.

Professor Black picked up the box.

"Ah, Miss Marchland. What an unpleasant surprise this is."

Mrs Whitehead clasped Viola's chin in her hand, lifted up her face and slipped her goggles onto her forehead. She glared at Viola's eye patch. "Not Miss Marchland?"

"The one-eyed doctor!" Professor Black drew in a sharp breath. The box thudded on the desk. "She's a known associate of Sir Archibald, works with Collins in the Police morgue."

Mrs Whitehead sneered. "You were supposed to ensure all of Huntington-Smythe's associates were accounted for."

"She was considered of no consequence," said the Professor. "After all, what can a woman do?"

"You little– " Viola lunged forward.

Mrs Whitehead pushed her back into the chair, glared at Professor Black and raised her hand to him.

"Am I of no consequence?" she hissed.

Professor Black flinched and darted to the opposite side of the desk.

"What can we do?" he mumbled.

"We do nothing."

A crack of splintering wood echoed down the hallway.

Mrs Whitehead lowered her hand. "You deal with her. There will be no loose ends. I trust you can perform that simple task?" She picked up the box, turned on her heel and strode out of the room. The door clicked shut behind her.

Professor Black circled around the desk and positioned himself between Viola and the door.

"How could you sell your soul to the likes of The Society?" asked Viola.

Professor Black avoided her gaze. "You don't say no to The Society."

Viola shook her head. "I'd never sell my soul to the Men in Grey. Never."

"You don't understand. I had no choice. The Royal Society refused to fund my experiments. They laughed at me. I needed the money to prove them wrong." He took a deep breath and opened the metal casket on the desk. "You must understand; you're a scientist." Glass rattled. He removed a vial of clear liquid and examined the label.

"It's used to sedate the target when a mask is made." He flicked off the stopper and plunged the syringe into the vial.

Viola scanned the floor for the pistol. A hint of gold glinted under the edge of the desk. She slowly stretched out her leg. Almost there. She pointed her toe and tapped the pistol closer.

Professor Black glanced at the syringe and frowned. "Of course, I'm not a physician." He drew more liquid into the syringe, and smiled at Viola. "I'm told it's like falling asleep."

Viola's breath quickened. She had an aversion to needles. She held her breath and lunged for the pistol.

The vial smashed on the desk. Professor Black charged forward with the syringe. Viola snatched up the pistol. She could not allow Mrs Whitehead to use the Chronosphere. Viola shot wildly in the Professor's direction. The syringe skittered along the floor in the opposite direction to the flailing Professor. She jumped to her feet, clutching the pouches tightly, dashed toward the door and slammed it shut behind her.

Tall brick walls lined the alley beside Professor Black's residence. Archibald rattled the gate blocking the way to the back yard. It was locked.

"Hurry up, Archie." Henry's leg brace clicked as he paced behind him. "Put your back into it, man."

Archibald retreated a couple of yards along the alley and charged the gate. A soft crack of wood broke the silence. A pain shot through his shoulder.

"Excellent," said Henry.

Archibald grimaced, clutched his arm and flexed his fingers. Nothing was broken. He peered at Henry, a vague shadow in the darkness. Archibald struggled to focus. Was that another shadow behind Henry? A distorted hump-backed figure loomed closer, raising a bar in the air.

"Henry, move."

The figure trotted closer. Archibald pushed Henry to one side; gears whined. The figure rushed at the gate. A thud, then a crack. It retreated a few steps.

"Don't just stand there," it scolded. "We've got to get in there; she'll need assistance."

"How do you know–?" Henry straightened his back.

"On three?" asked the stranger.

Archibald's shoulder throbbed. Pain shot along his arm. He flexed his fingers. He couldn't break through on his own. He had to help Viola. He joined the newcomer, glad of the assistance, and nodded. "One. Two..."

"Three." They dashed toward the gate in unison.

The gate splintered at the latch. Archibald tumbled into the yard, struggling to keep his balance. Henry's whirring footsteps followed them.

Archibald dusted shards of wood from his coat and peered into the darkness. "We should have brought some light," he said.

There was a clunk and hiss. A ghostly blue light erupted around them.

"Glad to be of assistance," said their new companion.

Archibald examined the illuminated figure beside him, a box-like pack harnessed to his back. A glass cylinder crackled with buzzing light, in his hand, revealing a green waistcoat. A badge glimmered on his chest: a lightning bolt set upon a brass cog. He flipped his dark hair out of his eyes and grinned.

"Excellent," said Archibald. "Shall we continue?"

"And you are?" asked Henry.

"Mr Chester." He shook Archibald's hand. "And you are Sir Archibald Huntington-Smythe?" He turned to face Henry. "You must be the fiancé? Doctor Collins, isn't it?"

"Pardon?" Henry's moustache twitched.

Mr Chester turned his light tube upward and skimmed the light across the sky and toward the wall. "Doctor Stewart has told me all about you," he said.

"I don't recall her mentioning you." Henry straightened and glared at Chester.

"She wasn't at liberty to." Chester seemed oblivious to Henry's displeasure. He surveyed the end of the yard, shone his light tube at the back corner of the house and moved closer to the wall.

"Why not?" Henry stood his ground.

Chester paused and sighed. "Have you not heard of the Secrets Act?" he asked.

"Of course. I've bloody well signed it!" Henry strode after him; the leg brace cogs whined and clicked in protest.

"Ah, yes. I'd forgotten," said Chester. "It seems we have been working on the same investigation."

Archibald eyed Chester. He worked for the Empire? What did he know? Surely Viola wouldn't have confided in him?

Henry stopped beside Chester and thrummed his fingers on the head of his cane. "How do you know Doctor Stewart?" he asked, not taking his eyes off him.

"She assisted me in an investigation, in Scotland." Chester

lifted a section of wood from the wall and shone the light into a cavity.

Archibald pushed his spectacles up his nose and regarded the two men: dark hair and moustaches, tailored waistcoats, determined posture. Two identical bucks intent on winning. But they were wasting time.

He took a deep breath. Viola was alone. In danger. And it was because of him. His footsteps rang through the yard as he marched ahead of them, toward the house into the darkness. His foot rammed into something solid; he tripped, slamming his hand down onto a concrete edge. He felt his way along the obstacle and onto the ground beneath his feet. Cobblestones? In the back yard?

He stood slowly and dusted off his palms. "I say, Henry, I've found something."

The light tube bobbed closer. It created a puddle of pale blue light at his feet, revealing cobblestoned paving and footpath.

"A street in the back yard?" asked Henry.

Archibald was already at the house, climbing the stairs to the door. "Be quick, man. We've wasted too much time."

Chester and Henry followed, dodged an unlit lamp post and joined him. The eerie blue light glowed on the knocker: a perfectly aligned brass lion's head. Faded paint flaked around it.

"A duplicate door?" Archibald ran a gloved finger along the edge of the door.

"And there's a hidden control box, with a pulley mechanism and pipes, in the wall," said Chester. "I think I've managed to turn off the gas. Darkness should slow the Professor down." He pointed to the heavens. "There's also a system of water pipes and light conduits leading up and over the yard."

Archibald's hand went to his jacket pocket. The newspaper? "An elaborate set up to replicate the front of the house?" he whispered.

"For what purpose?" asked Henry.

Archibald and Chester looked at each other. *Chester knew.* Archibald swallowed. But how? Viola would never betray him to a stranger.

A shot rang from inside the house.

"Viola!" Henry rushed forward and rattled the door handle. It was locked. He slammed his shoulder into the door. The knocker jiggled.

Chester shoved his crowbar into the doorjamb, just above the lock. All three men grabbed the bar and pushed. The door opened with a thunderous crack.

Henry pushed past them into the hallway. Archibald followed behind him. They stood in a hallway identical to that at the front of the house.

"Which way did the shot come from?" asked Henry.

The door slammed behind them.

Viola's footsteps padded on the carpet runner as she hurried along the hallway. This part of the house was unfamiliar. She had to find her way back to the front hall, to get her bearings so she could find the laboratory. Mrs Whitehead could not be allowed to use the Chronosphere.

She heard muffled voices ahead in the darkness. Perhaps she'd caught up with her. Viola turned the corner and froze. Four pale figures stood out from the background. She stepped back, adjusted her night goggles and peered around the corner.

A tall figure walked ahead of the group, carrying a gas lamp. Another covered the rear, brandishing a short pole with a curved end. One of the herded men walked with a limp.

"Keep moving." The rear-guard prodded the two men in front of him.

Viola crept closer, careful to stay out of the lamp light. Gears whirred faintly from the direction of the limping man. Henry? She clenched the pistol. She had one shot left. Her finger twitched. What if she missed? She'd proved a poor marksman in the past. She waited until the rear-guard separated from the group. She held her breath and pulled the trigger.

The leader halted, turned on his heel and grabbed Henry. A red stain spread on his comrade's trousers. Viola recognised Sir Archibald in the lamp light; she'd seen the two guards before - the Professor's butler and his footman. The butler thrust the lamp forward and yelled. The footman clutched his knee and crumpled to the ground and screamed, his face contorted in agony.

Viola gasped. She'd never shot anyone before - well, not successfully. Her hand trembled as she raised her pistol. Perhaps the butler wouldn't notice there were no bullets left. He flinched; Henry twisted free from his grip.

Sir Archibald grabbed Henry's cane and slammed it home into the butler's stomach and, with a practised swing, curved it around and brought it crashing down on the scoundrel's skull.

Henry teetered back against the wall, his leg brace clicking uncontrollably.

Sir Archibald raised the cane in the direction of the injured footman. He raised his hand and shook his head. Sir Archibald snatched up the dropped lamp and handed it, and the cane, to Henry, one eye still trained on the fallen footman. He grabbed the footman's arm and rolled him onto his side, undid his own cravat and wrapped it around the footman's wrists.

Viola lunged toward Henry, dodging the fallen men. She ran

her hand over his arms. "Are you injured?" she whispered to Henry.

Henry shook his head and pushed himself away from the wall. She dropped her hands and stepped back. "Henry, you promised.. ."

"But I–"

"*I* insisted we come." Sir Archibald stepped forward.

Viola raised an eyebrow. She didn't have time to discuss the issue; she had to make sure Mrs Whitehead didn't reach the laboratory first.

"We'll talk later." She glanced along the hall in the direction from which they'd come. "Where does it lead?" she asked.

"To the back of the house," replied Henry.

Viola's shoulders slumped. Not the direction she'd hoped; she needed to find the front hall. She pressed the mahogany box and file pouches into Sir Archibald's hands. "Here's the proof we were looking for."

"Viola..." Henry clasped her hand. "It's not safe."

"You're in no state for heroics," she kissed his hand, "and Sir Archibald needs to guard these ruffians." She slipped the night goggles over her eye patch. "Trust me, Henry," she whispered.

Henry released her hand and gave her his cane. "Be careful."

Viola smiled and turned to Sir Archibald. "Look after Henry."

Sir Archibald nodded.

"I have an assassination to stop." She gathered up her skirts and spun on her heel to face the opposite direction. "I have to find Mrs Whitehead before she uses the Chronosphere."

"But it's... " Sir Archibald's voice faded as Viola ran down the hall in search of the Professor's laboratory.

Viola watched the figure from behind a curiosity cabinet. A large carpet bag snagged on the ruffles of the figure's folded skirts. It had to be Mrs Whitehead; she would lead her to the laboratory. Until then, Viola watched and waited. She followed her quarry past the servants' stairs and into a wide hallway. Viola glanced along the hall. An Oriental vase sat on a hall table near the door at the far end. It was the front hall. Viola counted the doors and smiled. Mrs Whitehead had led her to the laboratory.

Viola hefted the cane in her hand. She could not allow Mrs Whitehead to access the Chronosphere. The Queen's life was in danger and Sir Archibald's reputation threatened. She *had* to stop Mrs Whitehead from entering the laboratory.

Viola held her breath, crept closer and raised the cane. Mrs Whitehead paused and turned. Viola squeezed her eye shut and swung the cane. For the Empire!

There was a crashing thud. She opened her eye. Pieces of shattered vase lay strewn amongst the crumpled skirts of the unconscious woman at her feet. The carpet bag lay on the floor, its contents scattered across the floor.

Viola gasped. Her fingers trembled as she removed her glove and held her hand under Mrs Whitehead's nostrils. A faint breath warmed her fingers. Viola sighed. Thank God, she was alive. Viola gathered up the document pouches and slipped them into the bag. Perhaps these would help save other unfortunates from the clutches of The Society? She snatched up the bag and rushed into the laboratory.

The laboratory was dark. Viola reached up to the nearest wall sconce and pulled the chain. The pipes remained silent. Viola frowned. The gas was off. Would there be any power to the Chronosphere?

She examined the room. The velvet pavilion covered the machine in the centre of the room. The control pedestal stood a few feet away. The tick of the antique grandfather clock near the doorway behind her echoed through the laboratory.

Viola placed the carpet bag next to the control pedestal. She glanced over the levers and dials on the panel. She'd assisted on enough of Sir Archibald's contraptions to know how to create a critical pressure surge. Her heart raced. Could she do it? Could she destroy another scientist's life work? She flexed her fingers. The Men in Grey had many agents; if she didn't, there would be someone else to take Mrs Whitehead's place.

She flicked a switch on the left of the panel. The velvet cloth jerked. Gears whirred. Chains ratcheted the cloth upward. Viola wiped her clammy hands on her skirt, cranked a dial on the right of the panel and pressed the button next to the dial. Her breaths quickened.

The Chronosphere hummed into life.

Viola closed her eye and concentrated on each breath, filling her lungs as deep as her stays would allow.

One.

Slow.

Two.

Deliberate.

Three.

Her pulse slowed. She opened her eye. Her fingers relaxed and dropped onto the next switch in the sequence.

A crackling buzz filled the room. Viola's night goggles flooded with light. She squinted in pain and flicked them onto her forehead. The room shone with an eerie blue glow, reflecting off the Chronosphere's rings, casting bright lines onto the walls like an enchanted cage.

"Stand aside, Doctor Stewart!"

Viola turned slowly. Mr Chester stared at the Chronosphere, as if enthralled. He held a light tube, a compact, more sophisticated version of the one she'd seen in the storage cellar at Marylebone Police Station. Blue lightning sparked from one end, filling the tube with light.

"This machine is now the property of the Department of Curiosities," he said.

"But I must stop the assassination," Viola flicked the penultimate lever and eyed the final toggle in the middle of the panel.

Mr Chester turned to Viola. The light tube cast long shadows over his face, shading his eyes and extending his brows over his forehead. "Step away, now."

"I thought you were in Her Majesty's employ?" asked Viola.

"I work for the good of the Empire," he replied. "And this machine could prove a valuable resource in its service."

"You said you would help me exonerate Sir Archibald," Viola's fingers nails dug into her palms. "You promised. One day, you said."

"Circumstances have changed. I can't allow you to meddle with the machine."

"You can always confiscate Professor Black's research notes. I'm sure they will contain all the technical specifications required."

"I already have them," Mr Chester smiled, "which is why I still want the machine. With a bit of work, our scientists could make it—"

A low grinding tumbled down from the ceiling. The walls

vibrated, filling the room with a ghost-like moaning.

"The machine?" hissed Mr Chester. "What have you done?"

Viola took a deep breath. For the Queen. She snapped the final toggle in position. And for you, Archie. She twisted the calendar dial to its limit - 1.9.9.9. She stepped back from the pedestal and watched the brass rings spin, with a gentle, hypnotic swish. It was done.

The rings spun faster and faster until they whined in protest. The Chronosphere trembled. Spurts of steam trickled from its base and seeped through the edges of the wooden wall panels.

Mr Chester stormed toward the pedestal and slammed the toggle back to its original position. The rings blurred. Puffs of grey smoke plunged into the spinning sphere of metal and disintegrated into the air.

"What have you done!" he growled. "We need that prototype."

Viola snatched up the carpet bag and stepped away from the pedestal.

He ran his hand over the panel. "There must be another switch." There was a loud click. He grinned.

The floor rumbled under their feet. The far wall shivered. One end disengaged from the side wall and scraped forward several feet. The floor shuddered.

Viola grabbed the edge of the pedestal to regain her balance. She met Mr Chester's gaze. There was a hint of panic in his eyes.

The room turned slowly clockwise, taking the far wall with it, concealing the other half of the room, and the laboratory door, behind it. They were trapped.

Machinery screamed beneath them. The room turned one hundred and eighty degrees. The blank wall was gone. In its place was a wall, with a duplicate door, complete with a ticking grandfather clock next to it.

Viola stared at the wall. The room had moved. The mechanics alone would be... She blinked. The. Room. Had. Moved. She stumbled forward, clutching the carpet bag to her chest. She fumbled at the doorknob. The door opened into the front hallway. Mrs Whitehead was gone. Had she escaped? Viola glanced along the hall. The front door hung at an odd angle. The curiosity cabinet stood on one side, an Oriental vase sat on the hall table on the other. But that was broken when...

"Two front halls?"

"And a duplicate street through the back door." Mr Chester was by her side.

"It's all counterfeit?" she asked.

Footsteps hurried along the hall toward them. Mr Chester lifted his light tube, revealing Sir Archibald and–

"Henry!" Viola ran up to him and threw her arms around him.

He hugged her and turned his head toward the rumbling noise. His muscles stiffened.

"What's wrong?" she whispered.

"Chester." Henry stepped back from Viola, his hand still clasping hers. "I wondered where you'd gotten to."

She turned to Sir Archibald. "The Chronosphere is counterfeit. The Professor is a fraud."

"I know," he replied.

"We have to leave." Viola moved toward the door and tugged at Henry's hand.

He didn't move.

"Henry?"

He released her hand.

Viola glanced at Mr Chester and back to Henry. "There's no time for posturing," she said.

Both men stood their ground.

A rumbling roar blasted the laboratory. The walls shuddered. Shards of metal embedded themselves into the wall behind Mr Chester. Smoke belched into the hall.

Viola grabbed Henry's hand. "I suggest we run."

The crisp scent of pine filled the air. Frosted tips sparkled on mistletoe sprigs hanging from the ceiling.

"I love Christmas," said Viola. "It reminds me of home. Father would always choose the tallest tree. Sometimes it was so tall the tip would bend over." She giggled. "And it was impossible to put the angel on top."

"We never had a tree when I was a boy." Paper rustled as Sir Archibald draped a paper chain over a bough.

"Then you shall have the honour of placing the angel when we're done." Viola clipped a miniature candle onto a branch of the tree. It jiggled; reflected gaslight danced on the ceiling. "Everything is so ...shiny." She sighed. "Anne and I used to take turns–" Viola caught her breath. The silver clip snapped her finger and the candle fell to the floor.

"You can't keep blaming yourself," whispered Sir Archibald.

Viola's wiped a tear from her cheek as she bent down to retrieve the candle. "You're correct." Viola took a deep breath. "I must live for the future, not dwell in the past."

She glanced in Henry's direction. He stood silently by the fire, arranging handmade Christmas cards amongst the holly trimming along the mantelpiece. His waistcoat peeked out from under his unbuttoned jacket - blue with a delicately stitched gold pattern. Viola smiled. It fit perfectly; A few weeks without Polly's chocolate cake had its benefits.

"Have you told him about Scotland?" asked Sir Archibald.

"Best not. He'll just worry. I was supposed to be recuperating."

"Secrets already?" Sir Archibald tsked. "And you're not even married yet."

Viola straightened one of the candles, avoiding his gaze.

"And will you tell him you were tricked by Professor Black and almost blackmailed by The Society?"

"Not I." He picked up piece of orange from the delicious morsels Polly had left on the table beside a jug of eggnog. "Besides, I've signed the Secrets Act."

"And Mr Chester said he will keep our names out of the report if I allow him to take credit for Mrs Whitehead's capture." Viola eyed the assortment of candied fruits on the tray, crusted with spots of sugar. She selected the last piece of fig and popped it into her mouth.

Sir Archibald chuckled. "Henry was eyeing the figs."

"Perhaps that's why he's sulking?" she said.

"He's doesn't want to attend Lady Calthorpe's party," Sir Archibald replied.

"Why ever not?" asked Viola.

Sir Archibald lowered his voice. "She keeps asking about the wedding. He doesn't know how to answer."

"Oh." Poor Henry. She hadn't thought her reluctance to set a date would have such repercussions.

"You should tell him how you feel, Viola." he whispered.

"But-" Viola clasped her hands.

"He'll surprise you." He patted her shoulder. "Live for the future, remember?"

Viola nodded, dusted grains of sugar from her bodice and joined Henry by the fireplace.

"We'll need to order a carriage if we are to arrive in time for

Lady Calthorpe's party," said Henry.

"Do you mind if we send our apologies?" She put her hand on his arm. "I've had too much excitement for one day."

"Are you certain?" Henry took her hand in his.

"I'm sure she will understand." Viola gazed into his bright blue eyes. Her heart fluttered. How could she have ever been distracted by the likes of Mr Chester?

"Excellent. I prefer small parties." Sir Archibald clapped his hands. "I've got a present for you, Viola." He pulled a brown paper package from behind a chair and presented it to her.

Viola slipped off the patterned ribbon, opened one end of the parcel and slipped out the contents - a magazine and a new copy of *A Christmas Carol*.I noticed your copy was getting worn," said Sir Archibald, "and I thought it fitting - ghosts of Christmas future, past, and all."

"And the magazine?" asked Henry.

"It's the story I promised Viola," replied Sir Archibald, "by that young writer I told you about, Bertie Wells."

Viola grinned.

"I have a present for you as well, Vi." Henry's eyes twinkled; he pressed a small parcel into her hands.

Viola unwrapped it: a decoratively-tooled purple leather journal with gilt-edged pages. Her name was embossed, in gold, on the front cover. A leather strap, with a fine gold lock, held it shut.

"It's a secret journal," said Henry, "to record your adventures." He dropped a small key on a chain, into her palm. "Only you have the key."

Viola's heart fluttered. It was the perfect gift. She hugged him. "I love you, Henry Collins."

The clock on the mantelpiece clicked. Sir Archibald held his breath. Viola counted the chimes: ... Ten. Eleven. Twelve.

Sir Archibald relaxed and smiled at her. "A toast?"

Viola picked up her cup of eggnog. "To being alive."

Acknowledgements

Thank you to my friends, David, Lynne, Sharon, Carole, Terry, James, and Zena, for their generosity and dedication. And thank you to Susan who lit the fire, insisting I write more stories.

Thank you to Terry Brown, of Dragonsblood Creations who supplied the beautiful gowns worn by the cover model, Zena Alliu.

Thank you for taking the time to read these shorts. If you enjoyed this book, please take a moment to leave a book review where you purchased this book or at Goodreads or Storygraph.

Tomorrow, When I die is a shorter Christmas adventure. It was first published as part of *The Illusioneer & Other Tales*, book three in *The Adventures of Viola Stewart* series, as well as separately as eBook - for those of you who love reading Christmas books. This books was published, for those of you who requested a print version.

Enjoy.

About the author

Karen J Carlisle lives in Adelaide with her family and the ghost of her ancient Devon Rex cat. She loves fantasy fiction, gardening, historical re-creation, and steampunk and can often be found plotting fantastical, piratic or airship adventures. Karen has always loved chocolate and rarely refuses a cup of tea. She is not keen on South Australian summers.

www.karenjcarlisle.com

You can support Karen at:
www.patreon.com/KarenJCarlisle
ko-fi.com/karenjcarlisle

Follow Karen at:
www.tiktok.com/@karenjcarlisle
www.youtube.com/@Karen-J-Carlisle
bsky.app/profile/karen-j.bsky.social
substack.com/@karenjcarlisle
www.instagram.com/karenjcarlisle
www.facebook.com/KarenJCarlisle

Where to buy Karen's books:
books2read.com/ap/nmAy7z/Karen-J-Carlisle

Leave a review at:
app.thestorygraph.com/profile/karenjcarlisle
www.goodreads.com/KarenJCarlisle

Sign up for Karen's newsletter:
karenjcarlisle.com/sign-up-email-list/

Other Titles by Karen J Carlisle

eBooks:
Doctor Jack & Other Tales
Eye of the Beholder & Other Tales
The Illusioneer & Other Tales
Tomorrow, When I Die: A Christmas Story
Blood Ties
Aunt Enid: Protector Extraordinaire
A Fey Tale
Twixtmas: An Aunt Enid Christmas Story
The Department of Curiosities
Mrs Hudson Investigates
The Case of the Forgotten Letter

eBook Short Story Collections:
Cogs and Conspiracies
With a Twist of the Nib
Another Twist of the Nib
Quarantine Reads

Also available in print:
Doctor Jack and Other Tales
Eye of the Beholder & Other Tales
The Illusioneer & Other Tales
Tomorrow, When I Die: A Christmas Story
Blood Ties
Aunt Enid: Protector Extraordinaire
A Fey Tale
Twixtmas: An Aunt Enid Christmas Story
The Department of Curiosities
Cogs and Conspiracies

Coming:
Secrets of the Empire
Book 2 The Department of Curiosities